The
Snow Tree

by Caroline Repchuk illustrated by Josephine Martin

DUTTON CHILDREN'S BOOKS

NEW YORK

*L*ittle Bear woke and the world was white.
"Where have all the colors gone?"
he cried, for he had never seen such a white
and wintry world before.
But the wind only answered with silence.

*T*hen out of the snow came Lynx.
He held orange leaves in his mouth
"For the Snow Tree," he explained.
"So we will remember the warm
glow of fall and the burning sunset
of an evening sky."

*N*ext came Squirrel. She carried scarlet berries and laid them softly at Little Bear's feet. They glistened like drops of blood against the snow. "To remind us of flowers and fruits from the forests and fields," she said.

Blue Jay flew down with feathers held
firmly in his beak.
"It's all I have to give," he said.
"But these feathers are as blue as the summer
sky and the rolling waters of the river."

From deep inside the frozen forest Mink appeared.

"Nature's finest," she declared, adding velvet fur to Bear's collection. "Brown like the rich earth beneath the snow."

Little Bear looked up as Raccoon came
padding softly through the snow and spread
fresh green shoots before him.
"My offering is to remind us of the green of
spring, of new life after the sleep of winter."

*R*eindeer moved slowly forward through the snow, with purple rock piled high upon his back. "Here is color that will endure forever," he said. "As purple as the mountains and the rolling clouds of thunder."

Bunting alighted on a nearby branch,
laden down with yellow cones.
"I carried all I could," she said:
"So we won't forget the yellow corn
that grows all summer long in the
fields beyond the forest."

*A*rctic Fox brought icicles that sparkled silver in the frosty light, like raindrops in the sunlight. "It is time to decorate the Snow Tree," she said. "And you, Little Bear, will guard this tree all winter long. Your black fur will remind us of night's velvet darkness."

Last of all came Moose.
A bright golden star hung
gleaming at his neck.
"Set this star high upon the
tree," he proclaimed.
"Let its light shine out to all
the creatures of the forest,
that they may gather to
celebrate the glory of
nature, and the beauty
of peace and friendship
this Christmas time."

Little Bear smiled as
he stood gazing at the glorious tree.

The colors were back.

For Ruth and Claire—J.M.

For Louise, who loves snow—C.R.

Text and illustrations copyright © 1996 by The Templar Company plc
All rights reserved.

CIP Data is available.

Published in the United States 1997 by Dutton Children's Books,
a division of Penguin Books USA Inc.
345 Hudson Street, New York, New York 10014

Originally published in Berkeley, California, 1996 by The Nature Company.

Devised and produced by The Templar Company plc, Surrey, Great Britain.

Calligraphy by Carole Thomann
Designed by Mike Jolley
Edited by A. J. Wood

Printed in Singapore
ISBN 0-525-45903-0
4 6 8 10 9 7 5